The Collector of Treasures

Published by ViVa Books

PO Box 28510, Kensington, 2101, South Africa

First published 1995
Reprinted 1996
Reprinted 1999
Reprinted 2002
© Copyright Bessie Head 1977
This story was first published in Ms Magazine (5.12) 1977 and
is currently in the short story collection *The Collector of
Treasures*, Heinemann African Writers Series.

With acknowledgement to the National English Literary
Museum, Grahamstown, South Africa, for supplying the
photograph of Bessie Head. © Copyright Vanda van Speyk.

ISBN 1 874932 16 6

Reproduction by Remata Bureau and Printers, Midrand
Printed by Pinetown Printers (Pty) Ltd. 16 Ivy Road, Pinetown 3600

The Collector of Treasures

by Bessie Head

Adapted by Chris van Wyk

Illustrated by Renée Koch

BOOKS

Johannesburg

Botswana's long-term state prison was in the south of Botswana. To drive to the prison from the north of Botswana took a whole day.

The police van came from the northern village of Puleng. They had left Puleng at about nine that morning. All day the police van droned as it sped along the wide, dusty road towards the prison.

The police van drove past ploughed fields, grazing cattle, bushes and trees. The prisoner in the back of the van looked out through the wire mesh onto all these things. But life in the bush went on, ignoring the prisoner's staring eyes.

As the van rode on the prisoner felt, deep in her heart, the pain of being alone, a pain that she had never felt before. This pain hurt so much that slowly she fell forward into a heap. She felt nothing around her but the pain. The sun set, darkness fell all around, but the van drove on, not knowing the pain of the woman it carried, not caring.

Then, many hours later, an orange coloured light shone from far away. This light came from the new independence town of Gaborone and shone like a ghost. Then the truck drove onto tarred roads and past lights, shops and cinemas. And now the bush looked like a dark ghost from the bright lights of Gaborone.

But the prisoner in the van saw none of this.

And her body did not move as the van stopped outside the prison gates. Suddenly a light was shone onto her face giving her a fright. The policeman thought she was asleep and shouted:

'Wake up now. We have arrived.'

He struggled with the lock in the dark. But after a while he got the door open. The woman came painfully forward on her hands and knees.

Together the policeman and the woman walked up some stairs that led to the heavy iron prison door. The policeman knocked. The night duty warder opened the door just a little, then wider for them to enter. The warder took them to a small office.

'What do we have here?' the warder said.

'It's the husband murder case from Puleng,' the policeman said. He handed the warder a file.

The warder sat down at a table and began to write in a big record book.

He wrote down all the facts about the Puleng murder case:

Name of prisoner: Dikeledi Mokopi.

Charge: Murdering her husband.

Sentence: Life.

A wardress came into the office. The wardress took the prisoner to a small room and asked the prisoner to undress.

The wardress took the prisoner's clothes and gave her a green cotton dress. This was the prison uniform for women prisoners. The prisoner put on the dress.

'Do you have any money on you?' the wardress asked.

The prisoner shook her head.

'So, you have killed your husband, have you?' the wardress said with a smile. 'We have four other women in this prison who have also killed their husbands, so you will have good friends here. More and more women are killing their husbands these days. Come with me.'

The wardress led the way down a corridor. She turned left and came to an iron gate. She unlocked the gate and let the prisoner walk through first. She followed and locked the gate behind her.

They entered a courtyard with very high walls. On one side of the courtyard were toilets, showers and a cupboard. On the other side was a large, cemented room.

The wardress walked over to the cupboard. She unlocked the cupboard and took out some thick blankets which had a nice clean smell. She handed the blankets to the prisoner.

At the lower end of the courtyard was the door to the cell. The wardress walked up to this door, banged on it loudly and called out:

'I say, will you women in there light your candle!'

A voice inside the cell called out, 'all right,' and they could hear the scratching sound of a match being lit. The wardress took a key and opened the cell door. There were four women prisoners in the cell. They sat up and stared at the new prisoner as she spread her blankets on the ground.

The wardress went out of the cell and locked it. The four prisoners greeted their new friend.

'Where do you come from?' one of the women asked the new prisoner.

'From Puleng,' the new prisoner said.

One of the women then blew out the candle and they all went back to bed. The new prisoner pulled her blankets over her and then she too fell into a deep sleep. She could rest now, after a long, long journey.

The breakfast bell went off at six o'clock the next morning. The women moved about in their blankets and stood up. They shook out their blankets and rolled them up into neat bundles.

A wardress unlocked the the cell door. The women came out of the cell and went to the toilet in the courtyard.

Then there was a loud noise of buckets and plates. This noise came from the gate of the courtyard. Two male prisoners had brought the women their breakfast. The men gave each woman a plate of porridge and a mug of black tea. The women sat down on the cement floor and began to eat. The women looked at their new friend.

'Be careful,' one of the women said, 'there is no sugar in the tea. We always scrape the sugar off the porridge and put it in the tea.'

Dikeledi smiled. She had been so scared while she had been standing trial that she became very thin. Her skin was tight on her cheeks. The other woman smiled at Dikeledi. The woman was fat.

'My name is Kebonye,' said the woman. Then she introduced her friends to Dikeledi. 'That's Otsetswe, Galebwe and Monwana. What's your name?'

'Dikeledi Mokopi.'

'Why is it that you have such a sad name?' Kebonye said. 'Why did your parents have to name you tears?'

'My father died when I was born. My mother cried when he died. And I am named after my mother's tears. My mother died six years later and my uncle raised me.'

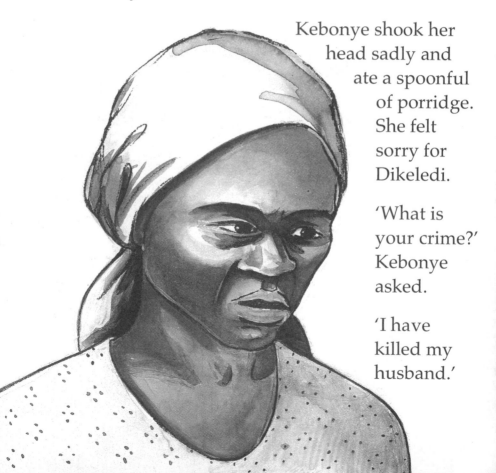

Kebonye shook her head sadly and ate a spoonful of porridge. She felt sorry for Dikeledi.

'What is your crime?' Kebonye asked.

'I have killed my husband.'

'We are all here for the same crime,' Kebonye said. 'Do you feel sorry about what you did?' she asked, smiling.

'Not really,' Dikeledi said.

'How did you kill your husband?'

'I cut off his special parts with a knife,' Dikeledi said.

'I did it with a razor,' Kebonye said. 'I have had a troubled life,' she said with a sigh.

The women ate their food without speaking for a while. Then Kebonye spoke.

'Our men don't think that we need tenderness and care,' she said. 'You know my husband used to kick me between the legs whenever he wanted that. Because of this I once lost a child. He wanted to sleep with me even when I was sick. And he would not take no for an answer. I once said to him he could even take another woman to sleep with when I was sick.'

Kebonye ate some porridge then carried on with her story.

'My husband was an education officer. Every year he used to suspend male teachers for making school girls pregnant. But he also used to make girls pregnant. The last time he did it the girl's parents were very angry and came to tell me about it. I said to them: "I have had enough of this. I will do something about it." So I killed him.'

The women finished their meal and washed their plates and cups. Then the wardress brought them buckets and a broom and they washed out their cell until there was not a speck of dust anywhere. That was how the wardress wanted it. The prison director was coming to inspect the cell. The women prisoners called the director the chief.

'You must be careful when the chief comes to inspect,' Kebonye told Dikeledi. 'Stand up straight and put your hands at your sides. If you don't he will stand here and swear at us.'

After the inspection the women were taken through a number of gates to a sunny prison yard with a high barbed-wire fence. This was where the prisoners did their daily work. They made goods which were sold to the public in the prison shop. The women made clothes. The men made furniture, shoes, and grew vegetables.

Dikeledi had many skills. She could knit, sew, and make baskets. All the women were knitting dresses and jerseys. Some were learners. They did their work slowly and made mistakes. They looked at Dikeledi with interest as she began to knit. She had soft hands that seemed as if there were no bones in them, hands that could caress with soft, gentle movements. From those hands came beautiful work.

By mid-morning Dikeledi had already knitted the front part of a jersey. The women all stopped to admire the beautiful pattern that Dikeledi had thought up herself.

'You are a gifted person,' Kebonye said admiring the jersey.

'All my friends say so,' Dikeledi said smiling. 'I am the woman whose thatch does not leak. Whenever my friends wanted to thatch their huts, they called me to help them. They never did it without me. I was always busy because it is with these hands that I fed and clothed my children. My husband left me after four years but I managed to feed my children. And if people did not have money to pay me, they gave me gifts.

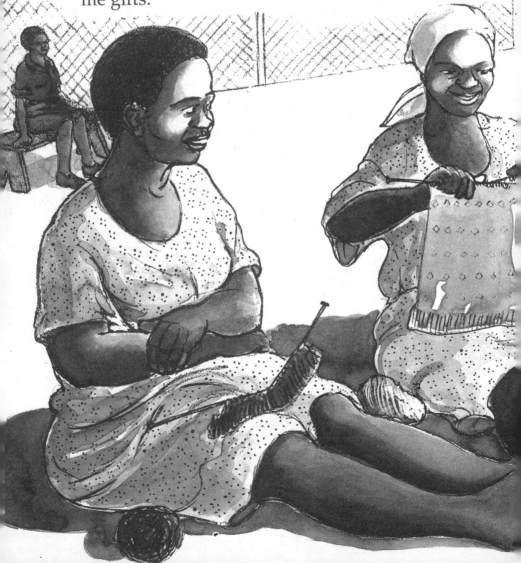

'It's not so bad here,' Kebonye said. 'When the prison sells our work they save some money for us.' Kebonye pointed to the jersey. 'If you work so well you can still earn money for your children. How many children do you have?'

'I have three sons.'

'Are they in good care?'

'Yes,' Dikeledi said.

Maybe Kebonye was beginning to get hungry now, because she suddenly began to talk about food.

'I like lunch here at the prison,' she said. 'It is the best meal of the day. We get samp and meat and vegetables.'

And so the women talked while they worked, and the day passed pleasantly. At sunset they were taken back to the cell and locked up for the night. They put their blankets down on the floor. Then they lit the candle and talked a little more. Before they blew out the candle to sleep, Dikeledi turned to her new friend, Kebonye.

'Thank you for all your kindness to me,' she said softly.

'We must help each other,' Kebonye said with a smile. 'This is an ugly world full of misery.'

And this is how the woman Dikeledi began part three of her unhappy and lonely life. A life that was sometimes more useless than ash. But sometimes she had found gold among those ashes. She had found people who loved her. And she had loved those people too. She smiled at Kebonye because she knew already that Kebonye was another of those people that she would grow to love deeply. She looked out for these people wherever she found herself. She was the collector of treasures.

There were only two kinds of men in Botswana. The first kind of man made people so unhappy that he could be called evil. This evil man was like a village dog chasing a bitch on heat. These dogs move about in packs of four or five. One dog always tries to get on top of the bitch and stop all the other dogs from enjoying the party. The other, unlucky dogs stand around while the top dog has his fun until he is too tired to have some more. This top dog thinks he is the only penis in the world. This kind of man lives and behaves like an animal. And just like an animal this kind of man does not look after the children that he makes.

This kind of man is to blame for the breakdown of family life in Botswana. He has been breaking up families for a long time in Botswana's history. He was here before the white man came to Africa. He lived according to the traditions of his tribe and obeyed the rules of his tribe. But he never asked himself if these rules or traditions were good or bad. He just accepted them.

When we study these laws we can see that they were made to make societies happy. But these laws were not always good for people. The chiefs made many mistakes. But one of the worst mistakes was to decide that men were better than women.

Today men still believe that they are better than women. And women suffer from this belief. But let us continue to study the man. He was destroyed even more when the white man took his land and made him work on the mines in South Africa. When this man became a miner he stopped believing in the old laws of his chiefs. And he stopped living with his wife and children as a family. This miner did not see his family for many months while he worked for a small wage to pay his taxes to the British Colonial government. This man then became the white man's 'boy' and a tool to dig up the gold on South Africa's mines.

But when independence came to Botswana it made this man worse not better. Independence brought more jobs and better pay and gave this man a chance to be a better person. This man could now live a happy life with his family; his wife and children. Men and women now had to use what they had inside them to build a good life for themselves. But when this man looked inside himself he found nothing; no courage, no new ideas, no determination. And when this man saw that he had nothing he began to destroy himself.

Garesego Mokopi was such a man. He was Dikeledi's husband. For four years, before independence, Garesego worked as a government clerk. Garesego's starting salary was R50 a month. Soon after independence his salary shot up to R200 a month, a good salary in those days. But even when Garesego was earning R50 a month he had a taste for drink and women. Now, with R200, he could afford these nice times.

Garesego left home and went around the village sleeping with one woman after another. Garesego had three sons with Dikeledi. Banabothe was four years old, Inalame was three and Motsomi was a year old. Garesego left Dikeledi to look after the children. Maybe he left her because he felt she was not an interesting woman. She could not read or write well and she was traditional. There were many new women around, women who could read books and talk about important things. Independence in Botswana had really brought the country some wonderful people.

There was another kind of man in the Botswana. This man had the power to build a better life for himself and his family. He looked inside himself and saw courage and strength and new ideas. And he used these things to build a new life. This kind of man loved his wife and children. He went on working and laughing and loving, day after day, like a river that keeps on flowing. Like a poem of love and beauty.

Paul Thebolo was such a man. Paul and his wife Kenalepe and their three children came to live in Puleng in 1966, the year of independence. Paul came to be the headmaster of a primary school in Puleng. The Thebolo family had to have a new home. They were given an empty piece of land next to Dikeledi's yard to build their new home.

When people live next door to each other they mean the whole world to each other. They help each other at all times and are always borrowing an onion, sugar or a spade from each other. Dikeledi Mokopi was interested, from the beginning, in her new neighbours.

Paul Thebolo was the first to appear. He came
with some workers to put up a fence. They put
up the fence quickly and did a very good job.
Dikeledi went over to meet Paul Thebolo and
she liked him from the start. Paul was a tall
man. He had large bones and moved about
slowly. He seemed to be at peace with himself.

When Paul stood still for a while to think,
sunlight crept into his eyes. And so sometimes
his eyes were the colour of shade, and
sometimes they were light brown.

Dikeledi walked up to Paul and greeted him.
He turned and smiled at her in a friendly way.
He told her that he and his wife had been
transferred from the village of Bobonong. His
wife and children were living with relatives in
Bobonong and they would come when the yard
was completed. Paul wanted his house to be
built quickly because school would start in a
month's time.

He said they would build mud huts first. Then
later they would build a house of bricks. His
wife would come in a few days with some
women to build the mud walls of the huts.

'I would like to offer my help,' said Dikeledi. 'If
we start early in the morning and there are
about six of us we can build the walls in a week.
If you want one of the roofs done in woman's
thatch, I can do it. All my friends know that I
am the woman whose thatch does not leak.'

Paul Thebolo smiled. He said that he would tell his wife that Dikeledi would like to help.

'You will like my wife when you meet her,' said Paul. 'She is very friendly and everyone likes her.'

Dikeledi walked back to her own hut with a happy heart. She did not have many visitors. Her relatives never visited her. They thought that since her husband had left her she would ask them for food or money.

The only people who visited her were people who did business with her. She made dresses for their children and jerseys for the winter. When she did not have any orders she made baskets which she sold. This is how she supported herself and her three children. But she was lonely for real friends.

Soon Dikeledi met Paul's wife. And she was lovely and friendly, just as Paul had said. She was tall and thin and full of life. She was a very happy woman and every day she showed how happy she was.

The six women built the mud walls of the huts in one week. Two weeks later the thatched roofs were completed. The Thebolo family moved into their new home. And Dikeledi Mokopi moved into one of the happiest times of her life. The Thebolo family became her friends. But they were not ordinary friends. They were friends who filled each other's lives with new and wonderful things to do and think about.

Soon Dikeledi and Kenalepe were as close as sisters to each other. They shared food, jokes and housework. And Kenalepe wanted more and more dresses for her three little girls.

Dikeledi made all the dresses and jerseys her friend wanted. But she refused to be paid for her work.

'Why won't you take the money?' Kenalepe asked her.

'Because you do so much for me and my children,' Dikeledi said.

But Paul Thebolo wanted to pay her in some way. And so, every time Dikeledi made a dress or jersey for the Thebolo family, Paul gave her some groceries. And this is how, for a few years, Dikeledi always had what she needed in the home: mealie meal, sugar, tea, powdered milk, and cooking oil.

Kenalepe was the kind of woman who made everyone around her happy, who made people feel that it was good to be alive. Many women from the village came to talk and laugh with her. And many of these women became Dikeledi's customers. Soon Dikeledi had so much work that she had to buy another sewing machine and employ a helper.

Dikeledi and Kenalepe did everything together. They went to funerals, weddings and parties together. And when they were not working they told each other their deepest secrets. Soon each knew everything about the other's life.

'You are a lucky someone,' Dikeledi told her friend one day. 'Not every woman has the gift of a husband like Paul.'

'Oh yes,' Kenalepe said happily. 'He is an honest somebody.' But Kenalepe knew that there were things that made Dikeledi unhappy.

'But why did you marry a man like Garesego?' she asked. 'I looked at him when you pointed him out to me near the shops the other day.

And I could just see that he is the kind of man
who sleeps around.'

'I think I mostly wanted to get out of my uncle's yard,' Dikeledi said. 'I never liked my uncle. He was a rich man but he was cruel and selfish. He made me a servant and pushed me about. I went to live with my uncle when my mother died. I was only six years old. It was not a happy life. All my uncle's children treated me badly because I was their servant. Uncle paid for my schooling for six years. Then he said I must leave school.'

'I was not happy to leave school. As you know, learning opens up the world for you. Garesego was my uncle's friend, and he was the only man who asked to marry me. The two of them talked about it, and then my uncle said to me: "You better marry Garesego because you're just hanging around here like a chain around my neck." I did marry Garesego, just to get away from that cruel uncle of mine. Garesego said he wanted to marry me, not an educated woman. He said educated women were stubborn and wanted to control men.'

'Soon Garesego began to run around. But, really, I did not even complain. I am not like other women who chase their husband's girlfriends from one hut to the other and beat them up. The man just runs into another hut, that's all. So you don't really win. I did not beat up any of Garesego's girlfriends. I am happy with my children. They are a blessing to me.'

'Oh, it isn't enough,' Kenalepe said, shaking her head in sympathy for her friend. 'I am surprised at how life shares its gifts among people. Some people get too much, others get nothing. I have always been lucky in life. One day my parents will visit me, then you'll see how much they love me. Paul is just the same. He takes care of everything so that I never have even a day of worry.'

And Paul also had as many friends as his wife. Paul and Kenalepe had visitors every night. Men who could not read or write came to visit Paul. They wanted him to help them fill in their tax forms or write letters for them. His own teacher friends also came to visit. They wanted to talk politics with Paul. They always had

something interesting to talk about now that
Botswana was independent.

Kenalepe and Dikeledi listened to the men talk. They were always very interested in what the men said, but they never joined in the debates. But the next day the two women would have their own debates about what they had heard.

'Men's minds travel wildly and boldly,' Kenalepe said. 'It makes me shiver the way they criticise our new government. Did you hear what Petros said last night? He said he knows all those bastards who now run the country and they are all just a lot of crooks who would pull a lot of dirty tricks. Oh, I shivered when he said that.

'The way they talk about the government makes you feel in your bones that this world is not a safe place. In the old days, when we didn't have governments, the world was safer. And Lentswe said only a few people in England control the riches of that whole country while the rest of the people in England starve. He said this was wrong but that communism would make it right.

'I could see from the way they talked that our government does not like communism. I trembled so much at the things they said ...' She laughed. Then she said proudly: 'When Paul talks to his friends he always says: "The British only ruled us for eighty years". Paul is so fond of saying that. I wonder why.'

And this is how Dikeledi began to learn many new things about life. There was so much to learn that she even forgot about her own empty life.

'You must find another man,' Kenalepe said one day. 'It's not good for a woman to live alone.'

'Another man?' said Dikeledi sadly. 'I like my life the way it is now. If I looked for another man I would be looking for trouble. Right now my life is all in order. My eldest son is at school and I can pay the school fees. That's all I really care about.'

'What I mean,' Kenalepe said with a smile. 'We are also here to make love and enjoy it.'

'Oh I never really liked it,' said Dikeledi. 'It was not at all nice with Garesego and now I don't like it at all.'

'What do you mean?' Kenalepe asked wide-eyed.

'I mean it was just jump on and jump off and I used to wonder what it was all about.'

'You mean Garesego was like that!' Kenalepe said surprised. 'That's just like a cock hopping from hen to hen. I wonder what he is doing with all those women. I'm sure they are all just after his money and so they tell him he's a good lover.' She stopped talking for a while. And then she added seriously: 'That's a good reason why you should find another man. Oh, if you knew what it was really like you would want it, I can tell you. Sometimes I think I enjoy making love too much. Paul knows a lot about all that. And he always has some new trick to surprise me. He has a certain way of smiling when he has thought up something new. Then I shiver a little and say to myself: Ha, what is Paul going to do tonight?'

Kenalepe stopped talking and gave her friend a naughty smile.

'I can lend Paul to you if you like,' she said.

Dikeledi's eyes went wide open with shock and she shook her head. But before she could say anything, Kenalepe stopped her by holding up her hand.

'I would do it because I have never in my life had a friend like you before,' Kenalepe said. 'A friend whom I trust so much.' Then she added: 'Paul had other girls before he married me, so it is not a strange thing to him. And you don't have to worry about getting pregnant. Paul knows how to take care of that. We used to make love before we were married and I never got pregnant. I don't mind lending him to you because I am going to have another baby and I don't feel well these days.'

Dikeledi stared at the ground for a long time. Then she looked up at her friend with tears in her eyes.

'I cannot accept such a gift from you,' she said, deeply moved by her friend's offer. 'But if you are ill I will wash for you and cook for you.'

But Kenalepe did not forget her kind offer to her friend. That same night she told Paul about it.

Paul was shocked. He didn't know what to say. Then he just laughed and laughed.

'Why are you laughing like that?' Kenalepe asked.

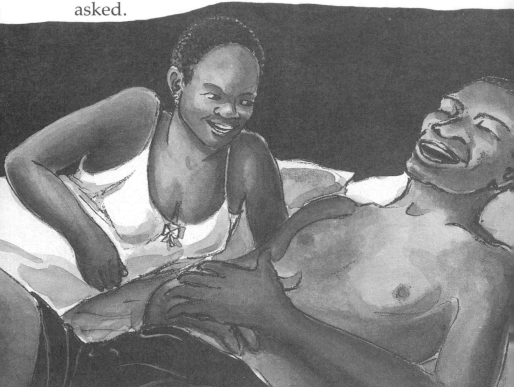

He laughed some more. Then he stopped laughing and became serious. He lay in bed thinking. When Kenalepe asked him what he was thinking about, he just said: 'I don't want to tell you all my secrets. I want to keep some of them to myself.'

The next day Kenalepe told her friend what had happened.

'But what does he mean when he says he wants to keep some of his secrets to himself?' said Kenalepe.

'He loves you very much,' Dikeledi said. 'He loves you so much that it hurts him to say how much, so he rather keeps quiet.'

Soon after this Kenalepe had a miscarriage and had to stay in hospital. Dikeledi kept her promise to her friend to wash and cook. She looked after her own house and her friend's house. She fed the Thebolo children and kept everything in order.

Kenalepe did not like the food she got at the hospital. So every day Dikeledi bought eggs and chickens. She cooked them and took them to Kenalepe.

One evening, after Dikeledi had dished up supper for the Thebolo children, a customer came. Dikeledi had sewn a wedding dress for the customer, but the customer wanted her to make a small alteration. Dikeledi had to do the alteration that night as the wedding was to take place the next day.

She left the Thebolo children sitting around the fire and went to her own home to work on the dress. An hour later, the alteration was finished and her own children were fast asleep. She went back to the Thebolo yard to see if everything was in order there. The children were all fast asleep and their dirty plates lay on the floor around the fire. The hut which Paul and Kenalepe shared was in darkness. It meant that Paul had gone to visit his wife in hospital as he did every evening, and he wasn't back yet. Dikeledi picked up all the plates and washed them in a dish. Then she took the dish of dirty water and threw it on the red coals of the fire outside.

Dikeledi piled the clean plates on top of each other and took them to the hut which was used as a kitchen. Just then Paul Thebolo came into the yard. He saw the light of the lamp in the kitchen and saw someone moving about there. He walked over to the kitchen and stopped in the doorway.

'What are you doing now, Mma-Banabothe?' He called her tenderly by the name of her eldest son, Banabothe.

'I know very well what I am doing,' Dikeledi said happily. She turned around to tell Paul that it was not a good thing to leave dirty dishes standing overnight but her mouth went wide open with surprise. Paul was looking at her and in his eyes were two soft pools of light that shone like water. They looked at each other and something happened between them. It was a feeling which they both felt, and so sweet that it could not have been love.

'You are a very good woman, Mma-Banabothe,' he said softly.

These words came from his heart and he gave them to her as if they were a gift of gold. Only men like Paul Thebolo could offer such gifts.

She took these words and put them away in her own heart. She bowed before him in the traditional way and then walked quietly back to her own house.

Eight years passed for Dikeledi, eight years of peace and quiet, and work. And eight years of friendship with the Thebolo family.

But then something happened to break the peace. Banabothe had to write his primary school exams at the end of the year. These important exams made the boy serious about school. He stopped playing around so much. He brought his books home from school and told his mother he would like to study in the evenings. He wanted to pass with a 'Grade A' to please her. Dikeledi proudly told her friend Kenalepe about Banabothe.

'Banabothe is studying every night now,' she
said. 'He never really cared for school work
before. I am so pleased that I have even bought
him a lamp and put him in my own hut where
he can study in peace. Now we both sit up late
at night. I sew on buttons and fix dresses, and
he studies.'

Dikeledi opened a savings account at the post
office. She wanted to save some money for her
son's secondary school education. The school
fees were R85. Dikeledi saved as much as she

could. But at the end of the year she had only managed to save R65. She was short of R20. During the Christmas holidays Dikeledi heard good news. Banabothe had passed with a Grade A. Dikeledi went wild with joy.

What could she do? The two younger sons had already started school. She would never be able to pay all their fees. She decided to remind Garesego that he was the father of these children. She sometimes saw him passing through the village. But she had not spoken to him in eight years. Nor had he ever asked about his children. Sometimes he would wave to her, but that was all. To him she was a low form of life.

But one day he had to talk to this low form of life. She went to Garesego's office just as he was about to go out for lunch. Dikeledi had heard from people in the village that Garesego was now living with a married woman with children of her own. Garesego had thrown out her husband in a dirty fight of curses and insults. Such ugly fights were normal in the villages. Maybe the husband did not care about losing his wife in such a way. There were always women looking for a man, any man, as long as he looked like a man. Garesego's new lover liked to do strange things when she made love. She liked biting and scratching. This was what her old lovers said about her. Maybe this is why Garesego was now living with her; because he liked this biting and scratching.

Garesego Mokopi walked out of his office and looked at Dikeledi, his wife. He was not happy to see this ghost from his past. He knew that she had come to talk to him, so he walked up to her,

looking at his watch a few times. Like all the
new 'success men' of Botswana he had a big
stomach, his eyes were red and the smell of beer
and sex from the night before hung faintly
around him.

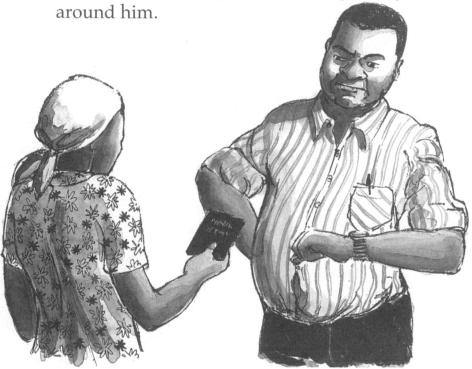

He showed with his eyes that they should walk
around to the back of the office block where they
could talk alone.

'You must hurry with what you want to say,' he
said. 'The lunch hour is very short. I have to be
back in the office by two.'

She could not tell him how proud she was of their son. He didn't care. So she just said:

'Garesego, I beg you to help me pay Banabothe's school fees for secondary school. He has passed with a Grade A. And, as you know, the school fees must be paid on the first day of school or else he will be turned away. I have struggled to save money the whole year but I am short of R20.'

She handed him her post office savings book. He looked at it and gave it back to her. Then Garesego smiled. It was an ugly smile, a smile that said: 'I know something about you, Dikeledi'.

'Why don't you ask Paul Thebolo for the money?' he said. 'Everyone knows he's keeping two homes and that you are his spare. Everyone knows about that full bag of corn he gives you every six months, so why can't he pay the school fees too?'

Dikeledi did not say anything. She just held her head up proudly, looked at him and walked away.

That afternoon Dikeledi went to her friend Kenalepe and told her what Garesego had said.

Kenalepe was angry.

'Garesego is a dirty pig!' she said. 'He thinks every man is like him. I am going to tell Paul about him, then he'll see something!'

Garesego did see something. But it was something he liked. Garesego was a whore who slept around. And just like a whore, he liked it when people in the village spoke about him. And that is why he smiled when he saw Paul Thebolo standing at the door where he lived with his lover.

Garesego was a troublemaker. This was not the
first time that an angry man had come to talk to
him.

'You bastard!' Paul Thebolo said, spitting out
the words. 'I do not sleep with your wife, do
you hear!'

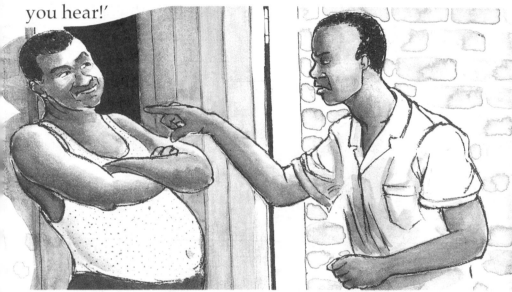

'Then why do you give her food every month?'
Garesego asked. 'Men only do that for women
they sleep with. They never do it for nothing.'

Paul Thebolo rested one hand against the wall.
He was half dizzy with anger and he said:

'You make life dirty, Garesego Mokopi. There is
nothing else in your life but dirt.

Mma-Banabothe makes clothes for my wife and children and she will never take money from me, so how must I pay her?'

'That only proves the story both ways,' Garesego said, pulling his mouth into an ugly smile. 'Women will only make clothes for men who sleep with them.'

Paul Thebolo punched him in the eye and

walked away. Garesego's eye swelled up. And every time someone asked him how it had happened, his reply was:

'It was done by my wife's lover, Paul Thebolo.'

The whole village began to talk about Garesego and Paul Thebolo. And that is just what Garesego wanted.

Garesego worked for the government. But he did not have a very important job. He was hidden away in a small office every day. He wanted to be as important as the President of the country. And now he felt important for a while. The village was talking about him. He enjoyed it and he decided to stir it up some more. He told everyone that he would pay the school fees of his lover's son, but he would not help with Banabothe's fees.

People in the village enjoyed hearing ugly stories about Paul Thebolo. He was a good, hard working, family man. And now they heard that he was sleeping with Dikeledi Mokopi. The village tongues wagged happily. But this did not stop them from wagging their fingers at Garesego.

'Your wife may be getting food from Paul Thebolo,' they said. 'But Paul cannot pay for your child's schooling too. Banabothe is your child, so it is your duty to care for him. And it's your fault if your wife takes another man. You left her alone all these years.'

So that story lasted two weeks. And people were happy to carry it from mouth to mouth.

They liked hearing that the good man Paul
Thebolo could also be bad, like everyone else.
But then suddenly something happened in that
village that made all the men tremble with
horror. And it was some weeks before they
could sleep with a woman.

Garesego's evil thoughts were to blame for what
happened to him. He really believed that
another man was sleeping with his wife, and he
was unhappy about this. He wanted to show
his wife that he was the man of her hut, not Paul
Thebolo. So, when he saw Banabothe in the
village one day he asked the boy to take a note
to his mother. The swelling in his eye had gone
down by then and he was ready for a new plan.

He told the boy to bring a reply. The note read:

> Dear Mother,
>
> I am coming home again so that you and I
> may make peace. Will you cook a meal for
> me and heat some water so that I can take a
> bath.
>
> Gare.

As Dikeledi read the note she began to shake with anger. She knew what the note meant: Garesego was coming home to have sex with her.

'Banabothe,' she said, 'will you play nearby. I want to think a bit, then I will send you to your father with the reply.'

She did try to think about this note. But her thoughts were not clear. There was something that she could not explain, even to herself. For all these years she had raised her three sons alone. She had seen many hard times, but the years had been almost holy to her. She had filled her life with treasures of kindness and love that people had given her, people like her friends Kenalepe and Paul. But now, Garesego, an evil man, wanted to take those treasures from her. And she wanted to keep them away from his dirty hands and his ugly, evil heart.

Her first thought was to take the children and run away from this village. But where would she go? And Garesego did not want a divorce.

She thought about ways to avoid him. But there was no way out, she would just have to face him. If she wrote back and told him not to put his foot in her yard, he would ignore her. Black women did not have the power to say such a thing to their husbands. Then she thought of an answer to her problem, and as she thought, a look of peace came over her face. She went into her hut and wrote a reply:

Sir,

I shall do everything as you want it.

Dikeledi.

That afternoon Banabothe ran back to his father with the reply. And all afternoon Dikeledi prepared food and heated some water for her husband. Garesego would be there at sunset. Kenalepe came into the yard in the afternoon and was surprised to see what was happening there. A large iron pot of water was boiling on a fire, and extra cooking pots were heating up.

Then Kenalepe saw her friend, Dikeledi. She was bending over a grinding stone. In her hand was a long kitchen knife which she used to cut meat. Dikeledi was slowly sharpening the knife on the stone. Kenalepe called to her friend, she wanted to speak to her. But when Dikeledi looked into her eyes Kenalepe could not say a word. There was a look in Dikeledi's eyes that Kenalepe had never seen before.

'I am preparing for Garesego,' Dikeledi said in a cold voice, 'he is coming home tonight.'

Kenalepe was scared by her friend's coldness. She turned and went back home. She told Paul what she had seen, and all afternoon Paul seemed worried. He kept doing things without thinking. He left a cup of tea to stand without drinking it, then he walked up and down lost in his own thoughts.

The Thebolos knew something was wrong next door, and as the afternoon grew, they grew quieter and quieter. Then at nine o'clock that night, they heard those loud, terrible screams.

Garesego came at sunset and found everything
ready for him as he had wanted it. He sat down
in the yard and prepared to have a good time.
He had brought a pack of beer along and began
to drink. Every now and then he looked
towards the Thebolo yard. The woman and her
children moved about in the yard. Paul Thebolo
was not around. Garesego was a happy man.
Once again he was king of his yard.

Dikeledi brought Garesego a dish of water to wash his hands. Then she served him his meal. She also gave the children their food and they ate in the yard away from their father. Then she told them to wash and go to bed. All the time Dikeledi watched her husband. He showed no interest in his children and thought only of himself.

If Garesego had shown just a little love for his children he might have stopped his wife from doing what she had planned to do. But he showed not even a sign that he cared for them. Nor did he show any feeling for Dikeledi. When she came to sit near him he did not bother to talk to her - or even look at her. He just went on eating, drinking his beer, and looking towards the Thebolo yard.

But Paul Thebolo did not come out, and soon it became too dark to see anything outside. Garesego was happy. He felt that he had won an important battle. And he could come and sit here in his yard every day until Paul Thebolo knew who was king of this household. And maybe Paul would become so angry that he would begin to swear or fight again. That would really be fun.

Dikeledi broke his pleasant thoughts with a question.

'Garesego, do you think you could help me with Banabothe's school fees?' she asked.

'Oh, I'll think about it,' he said.

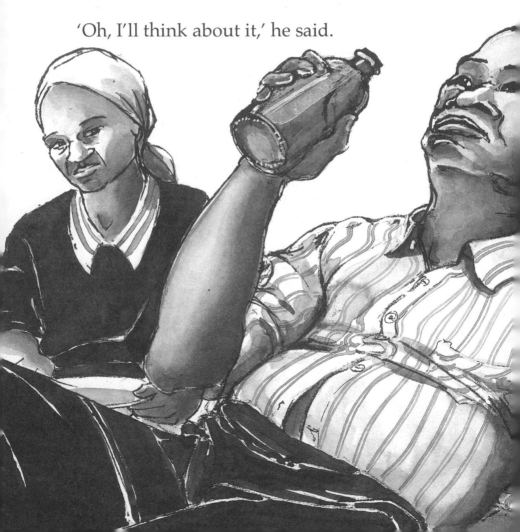

Dikeledi stood up and carried buckets of water into the hut. She poured the water into a tin bath so that Garesego could wash. While he washed Dikeledi washed the dishes and cleaned up around the hut. Then she went into the children's hut. They had played hard in the daytime and so they were already fast asleep. She knelt down by their sleeping mats and stared long and tenderly at her three sons. Then she blew out the lamp in their hut and went to her own hut. Garesego lay with his arms and legs spread out across the bed. It was clear that he thought only of himself and did not want to share the bed with anyone. Full of food and drink he was now fast asleep, lying on his back, naked.

Dikeledi picked up the tin bath and carried it out of the room. It fell to the floor with a loud noise. But the noise did not wake Garesego. Dikeledi came back into the hut and closed the door. Then she bent down and took out a cloth from under the bed. Slowly she unwrapped the cloth and there was the knife that she had sharpened that afternoon.

Dikeledi held Garesego's penis in her hand and, with one stroke, cut it off. Blood spurted across the bed. Garesego screamed and screamed in pain. Then all was silent. Dikeledi stood over her husband. She watched him closely as he shook, until he shook no more, until he was dead. There was a knock on the door and Dikeledi, after a long time, began to move. She opened the door. It was Banabothe. She just stared at him. The boy began to tremble.

'Mother,' he said in a frightened whisper, 'did I hear father cry?'

'I have killed him,' she said, waving her hand in the air. Then she said, 'Banabothe, go and call the police.'

The boy turned and ran into the night.

Paul and Kenalepe had also heard the screams. They came running into the hut. Kenalepe saw the dead man on the bed. She screamed and ran out. But Paul stood and silently looked at everything in the hut. Then he turned and looked at Dikeledi with pain in his eyes. After a long time he said: 'You don't have to worry about the children, Mma-Banabothe. I'll take them as my own and give them all a secondary school education.'

Word list

admiring (page 13) - to like the way something looks

alteration (pages 39, 40) - a change

caress (page 13) - to touch gently and lovingly

communism (page 33) - a system of government in which the workers rule the country

corridor (page 5) - a long passage with doors leading into many rooms

courtyard (pages 5, 6, 8) - a yard surrounded by walls

criticise (page 33) - to say what you do not like about the way something is done

debates (page 33) - discussions

determination (page 20) - when you are sure about what you want to do

divorce (page 55) - when a marriage is ended

droned (page 1) - made a low humming sound

faintly (page 46) - not strong

inspection (page 12) - when somebody looks very carefully at people or things

insults (page 45) - rude words that hurt somebody's feelings

introduced (page 9) - made somebody known to someone else

journey (page 8) - the distance that one travels

miscarriage (page 39) - when an unborn baby dies in its mother's womb

painfully (page 2) - feeling sore or hurt

proudly (pages 34, 42, 48) - having a good feeling about something which you or someone has done

raised (pages 10, 54) - brought up young children

relatives (pages 24, 25) - family members such as uncles or aunts

samp (page 16) - a corn grain that is eaten with beans and meat

savings account (pages 43, 47) - money that you have saved in the post office or a bank

seriously/serious (pages 35, 38, 42) - to treat as important and to think about carefully

shiver (pages 33, 35) - to shake from being cold or angry

shone (pages 1, 2, 41) - gave off light

staring, stared (pages 1, 6, 37, 61, 62) - looked for a long time at somebody or something

suspend (page 12) - to deprive somebody for a time of his job

sympathy (page 31) - the ability to share and understand other people's feelings

tenderness/tenderly (pages 11, 40, 61) - a loving way in which you treat someone

thatch (verb) (pages 13, 26) - to make a roof out of grass or reeds

thatch (noun) (pages 13, 24) - grass or reeds used to make a roof

traditional (pages 20, 42) - still using old ways and ideas

traditions (page 18) - the way of life of a nation

transferred (page 24) - moved from one place to another

treasures (pages 17, 54) - things or people that are highly valued

wagged (page 51) - moved up and down or from side to side

wonderful (pages 21, 26) - something that causes a feeling of surprise and admiration

Some facts about the writer

Bessie Head was born in
South Africa in 1937.
She was the daughter of
a rich white woman and
a black stable worker.
Bessie spent some of her
childhood in an
orphanage.

In 1958 she started work as a journalist on the
Golden City Post newspaper. While working as a
journalist she met and married Harold Head. They
had a child called Howard.

In 1964 Bessie left South Africa with her son to live
in Serowe in Botswana. The South African
government refused to give her a passport. This
meant that Bessie could never return to South
Africa. In Botswana she worked as a teacher. She
also wrote three books called *When Rains Clouds
Gather*, *Maru* and *A Question of Power*. Bessie wrote
about what it was like to be a woman in a society
where men dominated women. The stories people
in the village of Serowe told to Bessie made her
decide to write a book about their lives. *The Collector
of Treasures* is taken from her book of short stories
called *The Collector of Treasures*.

Bessie Head died in Serowe in 1986.